**E**ach Puffin Easy-to-Read book has a color-coded reading level to make book selection easy for parents and children. Because all children are unique in their reading development, Puffin's three levels make it easy for teachers and parents to find the right book to suit each individual child's reading readiness.

**Level 1:**  Short, simple sentences full of word repetition—plus clear visual clues to help children take the first important steps toward reading.

**Level 2:**  More words and longer sentences for children just beginning to read on their own.

**Level 3:**  Lively, fast-paced text—perfect for children who are reading on their own.

*"Readers aren't born, they're made.*
*Desire is planted—planted by*
*parents who work at it."*

—**Jim Trelease**, author of
*The Read-Aloud Handbook*

*For Jon Z., who will always*
*have a little scar*

PUFFIN BOOKS
Published by the Penguin Group
Penguin Books USA Inc., 375 Hudson Street, New York, New York 10014, U.S.A.
Penguin Books Ltd, 27 Wrights Lane, London W8 5TZ, England
Penguin Books Australia Ltd, Ringwood, Victoria, Australia
Penguin Books Canada Ltd, 10 Alcorn Avenue, Toronto, Ontario, Canada M4V 3B2
Penguin Books (N.Z.) Ltd, 182–190 Wairau Road, Auckland 10, New Zealand

Penguin Books Ltd, Registered Offices: Harmondsworth, Middlesex, England

First published in the United States of America by Viking Penguin,
a division of Penguin Books USA Inc., 1990
Published simultaneously in Puffin Books
Published in a Puffin Easy-to-Read edition, 1993

5  7  9  10  8  6

Text copyright © Harriet Ziefert, 1990
Illustrations copyright © Amy Aitken, 1990
All rights reserved

LIBRARY OF CONGRESS CATALOGING-IN-PUBLICATION DATA
Ziefert, Harriet.
Stiches / Harriet Ziefert;
pictures by Amy Aitken.   p.   cm. — (Puffin easy-to-read)
"Reading level 1.6" — T.p. verso.
"First published in the United States of America by Viking,
a division of Penguin Books USA Inc., 1990" — T.p. verso.
Summary: Jon falls off of his bicycle but is less than
enthusiastic about recieving treatment for the
cut on his forehead.
ISBN 0-14-036553-2
[1. Wounds and injuries—fiction.]
I. Aitken, Amy, ill.  II. Title.  III. Series.
PZ7.Z487Ss   1993
[E]—dc20   93-6553   CIP   AC

Reading Level 1.6

# Stitches

**Harriet Ziefert**
**Pictures by Amy Aitken**

PUFFIN BOOKS

"I fell! I fell!"
cried Jon.

"My head is bleeding!
My head is bleeding!"

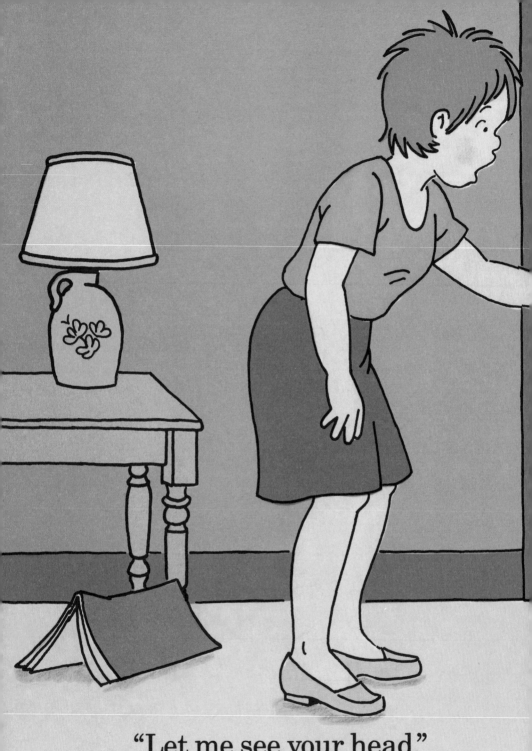

"Let me see your head,"
said Jon's mother.

"It's bleeding!
It's bleeding!"
cried Jon.

Jon's mother put a bandage
around his head.

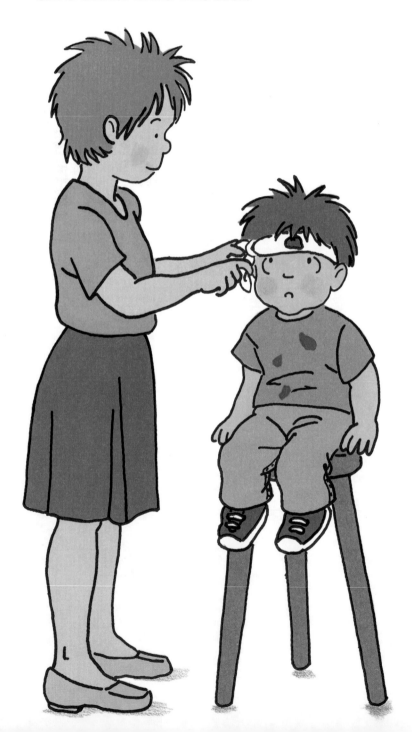

Then she took his hand and said,
"I want the doctor to see you."

"You need stitches,"
said the doctor.
"I don't want stitches!"
cried Jon.

"But you need stitches,"
said the doctor.
"If I put in stitches, then
you'll only have a little scar."

"Can you lie still—very still?"
asked the doctor. "Your mother
can hold your hand."

"Will it hurt?" asked Jon.

"I'll give you a shot so it won't hurt," said the doctor.

"I don't want a shot!" cried Jon.

"But I can't sew if I'm hurting you," said the doctor.

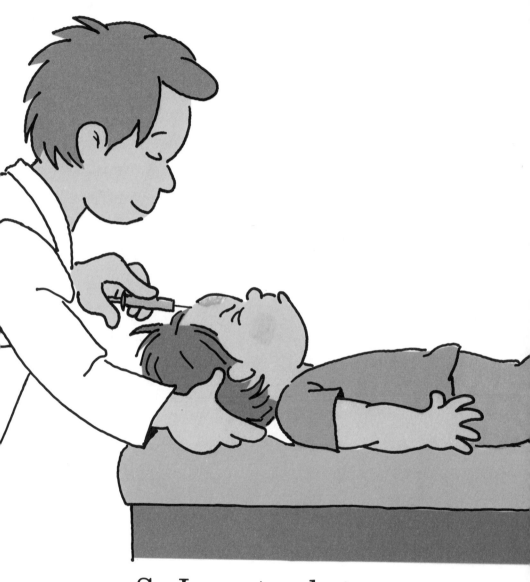

So Jon got a shot.
Ouch!

The doctor put in six stitches.
One...two...three...four...five...

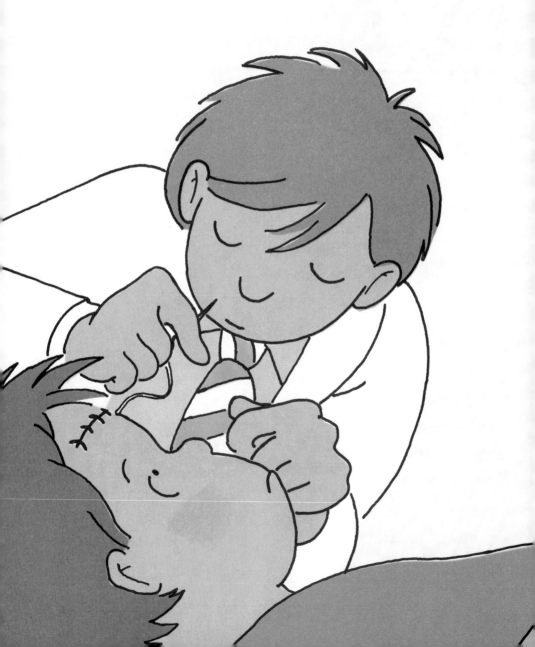

"Six!" said the doctor.
"All done!"

"I want to go home," said Jon.
"I want to go right now!"

"But you need a bandage,"
said the doctor.
"Then you can go home."

Jon was quiet in the car.
He didn't talk to his mother.

He wanted to get home.
He wanted to get to bed.

Jon lay in his bed.
"I don't like blood!" he said.
"And I don't like shots!
And I don't like stitches!"

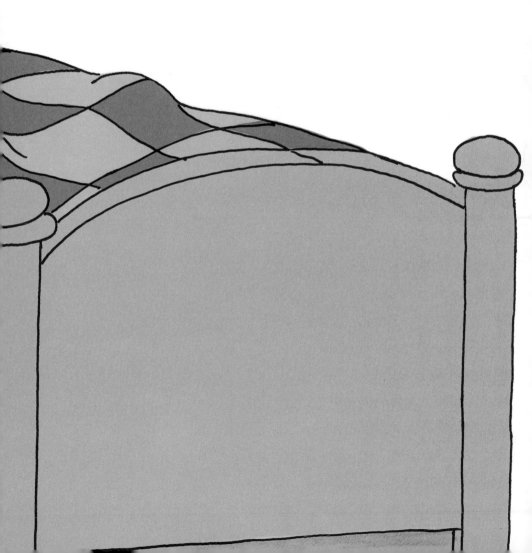

"Would you like chicken soup?"
asked his mother.
"No!" said Jon.

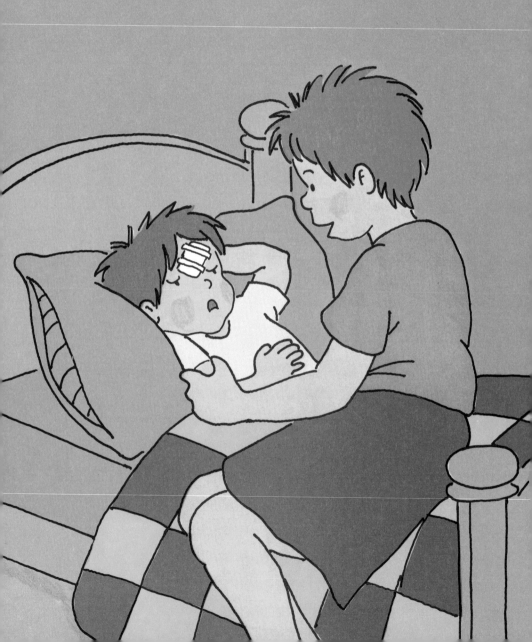

"Would you like ice cream?"
asked his mother.
"No!" said Jon.

"I don't know what you would
like," said Jon's mother.
"Please tell me."

"I'd like to see my friends,"
said Jon.

"Okay!" said his mother.
"I'll call them."

Jon's friends came over.
"What happened?" they asked.

Jon was happy to tell them.

"I fell off my bike," said Jon.
"There was blood everywhere!
I had to see a doctor."

"I got a shot! I didn't cry!
I lay still!
I got six stitches."

"And do you know what—
I'll always have a little scar!"